Why Life Is So Hard

978-93-5458-336-0

Adetunbi H Owolabi

pencil

ISBN 978-93-5458-338-4
© Adetunbi H Owolabi 2021
Published in India 2021 by Pencil

A brand of
One Point Six Technologies Pvt. Ltd.
123, Building J2, Shram Seva Premises,
Wadala Truck Terminal, Wadala (E)
Mumbai 400037, Maharashtra, INDIA
E connect@thepencilapp.com
W www.thepencilapp.com

Author biography

Adetunbi Hammed Owolabi is a Realtor , Construction Manager, Entrepreneur, Pan Africanist, Author and Global leader. He is the founder of Adetunbiowo & Co, a real estate and construction company. He is also the president of the International Youth Organization for peace and sustainability. Adetunbi's mission is to promote a positive philosophy of leadership, power of the people and ability to positively change their lives and generation. One of his visions is to propel generational blessings in Africa through desemination of knowledge through books, training, mentorship and other form of empowerment.

CONTENTS

Part 1 8

Chapter 1. WHY LIFE IS SO HARD 9

Chapter 2. HOW TO MANAGE LIFE'S HARDSHIPS
.... 19

Part 2 27

Chapter 3. SELF DISCOVERY 28

Chapter 4. HOW TO LIVE A PURPOSEFUL LIFE 35

Chapter 5. How Spirituality Facilitates Success 43

Chapter 6. The Importance of Being Focused 47

Chapter 7. NETWORKING AND MENTORING... 55

Chapter 8. LIFE IS A PROCESS 62

Chapter 9. EMOTIONAL INTELLIGENCE 65

Chapter 10. Financial Intelligence 72

connect With Author 76

Conclution. 77

Preface

PREFACE

We are in a part of the world where fear and lack of courage has replaced our strength and self-confidence.

Our overdependence on religion has made many weak mentally, lacking in ambition and drive. Our priorities have become misplaced and efforts are put in futile ventures all in a bid to attain success through the fastest means possible.

The essence of life has been greatly misunderstood. Positive attributes, which promote success, such as vision, hardwork, humility and patience are not given much emphasis. Also, the existence of love, support and a general goodwill among contemporaries is rare. Instead, envy, toxicity and unhealthy competitiveness is the order of the day.

There is a lot going on in our world today, which is affecting the people. The most detrimental of these challenges is the refusal of many to be realistic and reasonable in their approach to life.

Our mentalities are in need of a reorientation. We need to fix our minds on some simple truths. Central to this reorientation process is the acceptance of certain facts: Challenges are a part of life, life is a process, delays and mistakes are inevitable.

Miracles will not happen. Rather, you get out what you put

in. Also, important to note is that whatever the length of the process may be, focus should be more on learning and building a network rather than the achievement of the goal.

The importance of fixing the mindset of the people to inspire growth and success in them is the motivating force and inspiration for writing this book.
Life isn't meant to be easy; it is expected to be lived with understanding, patience and endurance so we can continue to thrive irrespective of what challenges we may be faced with

Introduction

INTRODUCTION

The objective of this book is to give a realistic perspective about life, it's challenges and ways to overcome these challenges so that we are able to lead progressive and fruitful lives.

Presenting a true representation of life and what it takes to be successful is extremely important especially in recent times, where there seems to be a prevalence in the misconception of success and the ways of achieving it. The sooner we are able to get a firm grip on the reality, the easier it will be for us to plan efficiently towards achieving and sustaining success.

This book is split in two parts. The first will discuss why life is hard and ways to manage the realities of the hardships and challenges while the second part will discuss effective measures to a sustainable success.

The hope is that we will be able to come to accept the truth about life and the requirements for success, which will make us better prepared for the realities of life and give us the requisite skills needed to be successful in our various life pursuits.

Part 1

Chapter 1. WHY LIFE IS SO HARD

The first step to understanding life is the acceptance that life is hard and that challenges are a part of life. The realization of this fact helps shape our mentality towards the challenges we face from an emotional approach to a practical one. Hence, we are able to be proactive.

In being proactive, we are able to be mentally alert and make allowances for contingencies because we expect to be faced with challenges. The popular saying which states that failing to plan is tantamount to planning to fail can be applied here.

There are so many reasons why life is hard. Some reasons are general and applicable to most people while others are more specific, depending on personal circumstances. However, the reasons that will be discussed are applicable to most people.

Constant comparison to others

Life is complex on its own. Adding competition with peers makes it even more complicated. While competition can be healthy, constant comparison to others is destructive. This is because there is someone who will always be doing better in one aspect or the other. Therfore, in obsessively looking outside of yourself, you will rob yourself of feelings of fulfilment that you are rightfully deserving of.

Unrealistic expectations

There's nothing better than being honest with yourself. Being honest about your strengths and weaknesses is very important because it enables you know where improvement is required. It also limits occurences of disappointment because you know not to involve yourself in ventures you are not qualified to take part in. Cutting your coat according to your cloth is a realistic approach to living life because it suggests living within our means in every aspect of our lives.

Emotional vs Practical

In order to tackle the problems that life throws our way, we have to be rational and clear-headed. Crying and sulking doesn't solve problems. The ability to see the problem for what it is and devise means to solve it can only happen when we employ a practical approach.

Fear of failure

Fear is a debilitating emotion. It paralyzes us and prevents us from living out our dreams and aspirations. Failure is not pleasing. It brings about dissatisfaction and disappointment. As such, it is perfectly normal to be fearful of experiencing failure. However, just as challenges are inevitable, failure and rejection too are inevitable. Accepting this fact and changing our mindset about failure is vital to our ability to be resilient and progressive.

Fear of not being accepted

It's a natural human emotion to want to be accepted by others. However, the need for acceptance can be problematic and self destructive. This is because needing to be accepted by others makes us put others before ourselves. Seeking to please others rather than ourselves is retrogressive and leads to hurt and lack of peace.

Putting others first

Putting others before ourselves is counter-productive. It emanates from a need to be accepted and being a people-pleaser. Do not be a yesman. It shows weakness and diffidence. It is not plausible to agree with others all the time. Be honest with yourself and others in a tactful and diplomatic manner. It is okay to say "no" and "no" is a complete sentence. You do not have to explain yourselves to others, especially to undeserving people, who are out only to take from you. What's the worst that can happen? Perhaps that fake friends stop speaking to us? That should be a pleasing development because it would mean that we will be emotionally and financially stable and free from negative influence.

It's important to note that if you want to give money, you must first have enough for yourself. If you want to give care and respect, you must also first care for yourself and respect yourself. In other words, you cannot give what you do not have. Therefore, putting yourself first is crucial in being able to be a pillar of support to others and being able to live the life of your dreams.

Taking failure personal

Just like challenges, failure and rejection are inevitable. As such, they are universal; everyone experiences them in one way or another. Therefore, there is no need to think yourself to be hapless or under spiritual attack or dumb when you experience failure or rejection. This would be an emotional reaction, which cannot solve the problem. Knowing that some others are experiencing same or even in worse situations should give us some solace and strength because others have experienced the same or worse and have come out stronger and better. Being proactive by investigating the cause of our setbacks, employing different approaches, seeking guidance and mentorship will yield more results than taking the failure personal, whinging and thinking ill of ourselves.

Poor choices

Though it has been established that life is hard, we can make it harder on ourselves when we fail to make good life choices. There are so many examples of choices that can be considered as poor. Some are the social circles we are a part of, not taking our academics seriously, gambling, drug and alcohol addictions etc. Such choices as these prevent us from setting right priorities, which will be beneficial to our growth. They serve as an impediment to our progress because they are distractions.

Money is hard to make

Though money is very easy to spend, it is difficult to make. Making money requires patience, consistency and discipline. There is always a need to reinvest in business to ensure growth and the bills simply do not stop coming. Sometimes, even when a business is profitable, the owner cannot benefit from profits as they would like because there are other more important decisions to make to ensure the sustenance of the business.

Quality relationships are hard to find

Finding people who are selfless is very difficult. This is because most people act in their self-interest. It's all about what they can get from you. This is the reason it's said that a wealthy man naturally has many friends. Finding people who genuinely care about your personal growth and success is very rare. For this reason, it's important to put yourself first always because chances are that no one else will.

Freedom is an illusion

Just as a perfect life is a myth, the concept of freedom is also an illusion. Religion and bad governance are the two major factors responsible for the limitation of freedom we experience, which in turn makes life unbearably difficult.

Religion is a contributing factor to the lack of creative thinking and freedom of expression in society. This is due to the restrictive and conservative nature of religious ideologies. The inherent lack of freedom of thought and fear of judgement and ostracism instils the fear of going against prescribed rules and regulations, thereby limiting the desire to break barriers and pursue goals vigorously.

Religiosity promotes an idea of 'us versus them'. It usually doesn't seek harmony, compromise, understanding, tolerance and love except for those within the same religion. In this way, most religious people live a life of hypocrisy, which in turn makes life difficult to enjoy.

The religious see their respective religions as supreme or the only possibility amongst other religions. This absence of respect and condescension towards people of other religions doesn't give room for a peaceful and stable environment where ideas and creativity can thrive.

On the contrary, it creates hostility and resentment.

Religion perpetuates ignorance. This is because to truly live, we must learn by seeking knowledge. Seeking the truth will not be encouraged by religious people if that truth contradicts or undermines their principles. Those that choose to enlighten themselves will be seen as rebellious and shunned by the group. In this way, it limits people's perception and suppresses their inquisitiveness.

Religion does not promote self development and free thinking because thinking is done on behalf of the flock by religious leaders. As such, there is no such thing as personal responsibility. Rules and regulations guiding every aspect of life are prescribed by the leaders and abided to by the followers. The absence of personal responsibility and individuality means that religion is a promoter of a herd mentality and emotional approach to dealing with practical life issues. Having such an ideology can make life more challenging.

Religion doesn't allow people live authentic lives because feelings and thoughts are suppressed. There is no room for spontaneity. All actions are assessed and reassessed before they are undertaken. The motivation for actions is not for self fulfilment or joy but rather, that they are payments for a place in heaven.

Apart from religious institutions, the government is another source by which creativity is stifled and life is made harder than it already is.

Bad governance and corruption causes societal decay and

stagnation.

The impact of bad governance i.e. poor infrastructure, lack of creativity, absence of competition and choice, poor quality education and healthcare, high cost of living, poor quality of goods, an uneven distribution of wealth, deplorable working conditions in the shadow economy, all contribute to slow development, which lowers the living standards of the population and contributes to their hardships.

From the points noted about the negative ramifications of bad governance, it's clear that the expedient approach to effecting societal change is for the private sector to take the lead, rather than hope on the government to take responsibility. Sure, this is easier said than done. However, all our years of waiting, trusting and hoping hasn't done us any good. The dearth of proper infrastructure and basic amenities will make any attempts at development extremely challenging. However, it can be done with proper planning, support and cooperation from all concerned. The way forward is for us to take ownership of our destinies instead of continuously leaving it to leaders who have done nothing but toy with our lives and that of future generations.

Provincial mentality

Narrow-mindedness can contribute to having difficult life experiences. This is because it limits your vision. There is nothing blissful about ignorance. Rather, ignorance is crippling. Ignorance is devoid of innovation and creativity. An ignorant person doesn't believe in self development and acquisition of skill and knowledge and in cases where they do, it is very limited. Therefore, having a provincial mentality doesn't allow us to keep up with the changing global environment. It doesn't foster progress but instead causes stagnation.

Inequality of resources and opportunities

Inequality is another fact of life. Even in communist societies, where the goal was to eliminate the class system, thereby promoting equality, a class system still existed. A class structure emerged through securing quality higher education, thereby making only a small group eligible for elite government positions. Apart from education, distinctions were made in terms of location. For example, migrant workers had a lower status than 'core' workers just as urban workers had a higher status than rural workers had. Communism has been used to illustrate the implausibility of equality even when we have the best intentions of ensuring it.

There will always be those who are born into wealthy families, who naturally have better opportunities than those from poor backgrounds. The countries in which we are born can also determine how difficult or relatively easy our lives may turn out. For example, residents of countries in Europe and North America, where social amenities are available, where the government is responsible and development is progressive can be sure to have an easier life than those in developing countries, such as Nigeria.

Therefore, it is little wonder that birth tourism and the 'brain drain' are prevalent in our society. Survival is a natural human instinct and people will go where they feel they have a better chance of thriving if they find their immediate surroundings inhabitable.

Lack of Love

Love is an emotion that is lacking in our society. In its place, what is prevalent is envy, hatred and selfishness. These negative emotions are the cause of the deterioration of our society and the failure of our governments. Abuse of power is rampant in every sphere of our society and we must do better in putting a check on this evil act.

While it is convenient to focus on selfish leaders, we must remember that the citizens outnumber the leaders. As such, if the citizens are positive towards one another, there will be a significant improvement in our society. We all have a part to play in showing care, concern and fairness to one another starting from our families, friendship circles, coworkers, employees and neighbours.

Difficulty in finding support

The most effective way to achieve a better society is through a mental reorientation. There needs to be more assistance and less resistance, more building up rather than tearing down. Abuse of power and privilege has eaten so deep into every sphere of our society, so much so that it has become normalized. It is important to encourage victims to speak up, and they can only be willing to do so if they are guaranteed support rather than blame. Likewise, the perpetrators need to be named and shamed in order to discourage others from engaging in such heinous acts.

Hatred

Hatred has eaten so deep into our society. Unhealthy competition is the order of the day. Many are willing to go to extraordinary lengths to tear others down and deprive them of sustenance. Our society has become a dog eat dog one, oftentimes feeling like a war zone. Even children are not spared the pervasive toxicity.

Negativity doesn't breed positivity so it's essential to stand on the right and give off energy you want back. For enduring rather than fleeting success, fairness, cordiality, sensibility and diligence will put you in better stead than negativity. For example, if there is a person you admire, rather than despise them for their ingenuity, it will be more productive and sensible to humble yourself and ask to be mentored.

Chapter 2. HOW TO MANAGE LIFE'S HARDSHIPS

Though there is no such thing as a perfect life i.e. one without challenges, there are ways by which we can manage life's hardships.

These are explained in the following sections.

Improve your appearance

It is said that we are addressed according to the way we are dressed. This simply means that our appearance and the way in which we present ourselves goes a long way in determining the type of attention we get and from whom we get it. Proper grooming is essential. Respecting yourself means that you take good care of yourself. However, having a pleasing appearance has nothing to do with wearing designer labels. It simply means that we must be neat and tidy regardless of whether we are dressed expensively or in second-hand clothing. Having a good appearance tells a lot about who we are and attracts people to us. It has the ability to open doors for us that would otherwise have been shut.

Improve the quality of your social circle

Birds of the same feather flock together. The company we keep tells a great deal about who we are as people. Like minds attract, so chances are our friends share a similar mentality to ours. The company we keep determines the type of choices we make and the trajectory of our lives.

Positive influences motivate us and inspire us to achieve greatness while negative influences derail us and distract us from being successful.

Make your own rules

Making your own rules stems from having an independent mind. Being able to think for yourself is very important because it is the mark of a leader. The ability to make your own rules comes from a good knowledge of yourself; what your strengths are and what your weaknesses are. It is crucial to be honest in your examination of yourself so that the rules you make can yield benefits.

For example, say there's a young man whose interests lie in carpentry, and in particular furniture making. Not only does he have a passion for furniture making, he has the capabilities of being an excellent furniture maker. With this conviction, after high school, he decides to forgo a traditional education at university and instead pursues a degree at a technical institute and interns under world-class furniture makers to gain experience and further develop his skills.

Deciding to follow such a path as described in the previous paragraph is an example of following an individual path because it is not the conventional approach. It is taking a decision based on our individual needs and goals in spite of what is popular. Needless to say, it requires confidence and self belief. The more popular option would be to get the university degree as a backup plan and then pursue passion afterwards.

Victor vs Victim

It is said that battles are first won in the mind. The way we assess and respond to our circumstances determines if we will end up being victorious over them or if we will remain victimized by them.

Having a victor mentality is important because it is a proactive and practical approach to life. A victor is one who is aware that challenges are bound to surface, someone who knows that the challenges are not an indication of laxity or a lack of acumen. A victor does not take setbacks personal but instead sees them as an opportunity for learning and development.

Victims are essentially the antithesis of victors. A victim sees challenges as a form of punishment and can even go as far as regarding obstacles as a spiritual attack. Victims hardly take responsibilty for their actions, instead they blame other forces, seen and unseen for their problems.

Victims waste so much time moping, complaining and getting emotional. They fail to plan for unforseen contingencies so are taken by surprise when they occur.

In order to be successful in life, you must adopt the victor mentality, even in times when your self belief is not firm. You have no other option than to win so you must keep believing that you are a winner and are capable of overcoming every challenge that comes your way.

Patience

Patience is truly a virtue. Patience is the ability to be calm and trust that our efforts will yield fruit with time. Patience goes against the modern school of thought because today, instant gratification is the norm. People want quick results and so they rather opt for short cuts, which often lead to fleeting success. Patience on the other hand, is all about delayed gratification. Patience trusts in paying your dues and putting in the required efforts needed for self development. Patience is a vital characteristic necessary for enjoying enduring success.

Selfish isn't always bad

Just as was mentioned earlier, it is important to put yourselves first. This isn't only because no one else will put you first but because it is essential to your self development and progress. Selfishness is not always a negative trait. In this regard, it isn't. Rather, it is positive to be selfish about your determination to succeed because it means being motivated to seek knowledge and gain experiences that will be beneficial to your growth. It also means getting to know yourself and your capabilities and pouring all your energies and resources into developing these capabilities. Putting yourself first is essentially doing everything within your power, that is legal, to give yourself the best chance of being successful.

Stop faking it!

It's true that people sometimes fake it to protect themselves from wagging tongues but to go as far as living on credit to give people an erroneous perception of yourself is going too far. Faking it can be detrimental because it gives a misconception of who you really are and if no one knows the real you, those who would have been willing to help won't be able to because they would have no idea you need any assistance.

It must be said that this is by no means advocating being an open book and telling anyone who cares to listen about your struggles. However, there is a balance that can be struck between carrying yourself with dignity and being expressive about your search for an improved circumstance.

Self belief

Believing in yourself can mitigate the effects of a hard life. This is because self belief can serve as fuel to motivate and strengthen our resolve to become achievers. When all chips are down and you've given it all you can, self belief is what keeps you going. Self belief is what makes the difference between staying down and getting up and trying again. Resilience, perseverance, patience and individuality are all aspects of self belief. It will be impossible to face challenges and overcome them without belief in yourself.

Get rid of the slave mentality!

A slave is someone who is subserviant to another, who is in total control of the slave. A person can be a slave to money, religion, peer pressure, trends and fads, publicity, materialism etc. Whatever it is a person is a slave to is the master of the person.

There is no positive aspect to being a slave. Slaves do not have their own mind and so act based on outside influence. There is nothing more pathetic and pitiful than being a slave.

A slave to money will put profits before value and integrity.

A slave to religion will misinterpret religious text and place erroneous doctrines before self development and responsibility.

A slave to peer pressure will put friends before self and make decisions based on the approval of others.

A slave to trends will never be consistent because their objectives will change as the trends change. Such a person will go in whichever direction the wind is blowing.

A slave to publicity will have the wrong motive for actions taken. Everything will be done with a mind to gain attention and for feeding their ego. The intention or motive is the foundation on which we build.

Therefore, wrong intentions can lead us to having misplaced priorities.

A slave to materialism will fail to reinvest in business and instead be profligate with their financial resources. Such a person will squander all profits and even their capital on the purchase of luxury goods.

From the examples listed, it's clear that not having control of ourselves is destructive. We must be our own masters so that we can be in control of our destinies rather than sell ourselves cheaply to outside forces.

Discipline

Discipline is training that produces moral or mental improvement. Therefore, being disciplined yields benefits. The moral benefits that can be derived from being disciplined include contentment, integrity, patience, diligence, perseverance and honesty. Mentally, discipline causes us to be undeterred by the goings-on around us, instead it gives us the ability to remain focused on our individual journeys. The moral and mental strength derived from living a disciplined life are necessary aspects to being able to cope with the hardships of life.

Be choosy about who you take advice from
The online space and social media, in particular, has given rise to a plethora of motivational speakers and life coaches. While it is a welcome development to have access to a multitude of positive voices, it's important to be cautious about who we take advice from.

Firstly, not everyone who claims to be a life coach or motivational speaker actually has their life in order. Some live lives opposite to what they preach.

Secondly, not every advice, however good it sounds, is meant for everybody. We must learn to sieve the advice we receive and take those that apply to our particular circumstance and stage of life.

Thirdly, it's important to look beyond the eloquence of the speaker. All that glitters isn't gold. Does the person really walk the talk or are they faking it? No human is perfect but in choosing a mentor, we must look out for people with integrity, those that model positivity, people who are a representation of our aspirations. Seeing that our dreams can actually come to fruition will serve as a driving force to keep us motivated and continually striving for success.

Now that we have established that life is inherently riddled with challenges and discussed ways by which the effects of these difficulties can be mitigated, the hope is that there's now a realization that we are all capable of handling the hardships that come our way and that rather than fear being our primary emotion when faced with challenges, we will rather be calm and confident.

Being able to face the realities of the hardships and challenges of life will put us in a good position to plan towards a successful life. In order to enjoy enduring success, there are factors that must be taken into consideration. These will be discussed in the second part of the book.

Part 2

Chapter 3. SELF DISCOVERY

Who am I?

It's important to know who we are if we are to be successful in life. This is because the knowledge of our strengths, weaknesses, passions, dislikes and idiosyncrasies inform what career path will be suitable for us. The knowledge of self is also important because it is the foundation of self belief borne out of the knowledge of our capabilities. Knowing who you are enables you to have a firm footing in a world filled with distractions; it enables you to stay focused. Your principles are a product of who you are. Knowing who you are protects you from being enslaved by trends and peer pressure. Confidence and firmness are attributes that emanate from having a knowledge of yourself. As the only constant in life is change, who we are is also ever evolving.

What do I need?

Once you have knowledge of who you are, you can then begin to understand what matters most to you. Generally speaking, we all need the basics of shelter, clothing, food and healthcare. Beyond these, what we need depends on who we are and what appeals to us.

Just like who we are is bound to change with self development, our needs also change with time. For example, a new business owner may initially need to have the patronage of the residents of their immediate environment. However, with time, after that objective has been met, the need may change to expanding to neighbouring localities. Human needs are insatiable by nature. Therefore, it is expected to constantly review and re-evaluate our needs to suit of current circumstances.

What makes me happy?
Having an intimate knowledge of yourself and being honest about your findings will help determine what makes you happy. These are activities that bring you joy and fulfilment such that you wouldn't mind doing them even if you weren't getting paid a great deal of money.
Sometimes, it could be a feeling rather than an activity. For some it may be caring for people, for others it may be being able to express themselves creatively. These feelings can be channelled into a suitable career path. For example someone who derives pleasure from creative expression shouldn't choose banking as a career path. This is because banking follows prescribed methods and processes. The existence of a formal dress code may also be a turn off for such a person. Freelance writing or blogging may instead be a preferable path for a creative person.

What bothers me?

If we are not in tune with our inner selves, we wouldn't know to distinguish between what is appealing and otherwise. Instead, we will be sold to every suggestion and this can be time wasting and destructive. In knowing yourself and understanding what makes you happy, you would also be aware of what bothers you. These are the things we do not want to be a part of our lives. It's important to follow your intuition in this regard. Our body sensation usually will recoil and contract when we are faced with an undesirable situation. Our instincts are a way of our inner self communicating with us and so we must pay attention to them.

Reconcile with your past

In order to know where we're heading, we must know where we're coming from. It's important to make sense of our past so that we are free from being enslaved by it, consciously or otherwise. To a large degree, we are all shaped by our experiences, both good and bad, and so we sometimes act out of our prejudices rather than the reality of a situation.

For example, a person who was raised in a household where they were constantly criticized for being expressive will most likely grow up defensive and unwilling to express themselves. Though the reality of the present situation does not call for such a behaviour, it is exhibited regardless because the person has learned to guard themselves from criticism by keeping their thoughts to themselves. They have grown up to assume that they will be criticized if they express their opinions as they were in childhood.

Having the courage to explore our past enables us to deal with unresolved trauma and gives us a deeper understanding as to the reasons we behave the way we do or react to certain situations in a peculiar manner. We will benefit by being better able to understand ourselves and freeing ourselves from the baggage we were unknowingly carrying around.

Be your own person

Being your true self is only possible after you are able to free yourself from the bondage of the past. Examples of traits developed from our past that tend to hold us captive include toxic internalized thought processes, inherited behavioural traits from parents and defence mechanisms used to cope with our former circumstances. These are described as bondage because they do not allow us to evolve as we become a slave to them. The saddest part is that we are often not aware that they have such a strong hold on us.

Removing the shackles of our past is extremely important in discovering who we really are. Who we thought we were was not an accurate representation because it was informed in a large part by our past experiences. Now being free mentally and emotionally, we are now able to truly get to know ourselves without the cloud of our pasts hovering over us.

Seek truth

Seeking the truth can be a daunting exercise. This is because we may find that the truth contradicts our beliefs and all we have always held dear. However scary it may be, we must always be willing to discover the truth of any and every thing because in doing so, we are able to have an unbiased understanding, which eventually gives us peace and freedom of thought.

For example, learning the truth about life and it's hardships and challenges makes it easier for us to navigate through life. The easier we are able to deal with the challenges we are faced with, the better chances we have at being successful.

Seek meaning

Seeking meaning is just as important as seeking truth. Seeking meaning is essentially finding a purpose. A purpose is the reason for your existence, what you want to dedicate your life to. Your purpose must also not be a singular activity, you can have more than one purpose. What's most important is that you are intentional about making the different activities cohesive so as to maintain focus. Finding your purpose is personal; what means the world to one person may seem frivolous to the next. The importance of knowing yourself comes in here because it's important to be firm in your resolve about your purpose so that distractions and self doubt do not thwart your path towards success.

Recognize your potentials

In getting to know yourself, you would be able to understand your capabilities. Your strengths and weaknesses inform what sort of activities you will potentially thrive in and gives you an insight on how and where to focus your energies.

Your potentials are those positive attributes that set you apart from others. They are abilities that when developed, can contribute to success. Recognizing that you have potential is a good feeling as it gives an inner power, from which flows positive thoughts about ourselves. It also gives us the self assertion, confidence and motivation to strive for our goals

Be compassionate

It is truly more blessed to give than to receive. Giving of our time is an important aspect of getting to know who we are and living a purposeful life. Not only do we benefit from improving our physical, mental and emotional well-being from service to others, being compassionate adds value and meaning to our lives. Mahatma Gandhi sums the importance of compassion and generosity when he said, "the best way to find yourself is to lose yourself in the service of others."

Value relationships

While we cannot choose our family members, we certainly can choose our friends, who may or may not include members of our family. The choices of friendships we make and people we choose to be acquainted with says a lot about who we are and how we perceive ourselves. It also has a correlation to what we envision for our future.

Therefore, it is important to choose wisely as friendships can determine how successful or stagnant our lives turn out to be. We should choose people who are positive influences; those that inspire, support, protect, radiate happiness and advise us rightly.

Importance of stillness

Stillness is very important as it is the key to communing with your inner self. Self discovery cannot be achieved by constantly being in a crowd. From time to time, it's important to get away from the noise in order to connect or reconnect with yourself. Stillness is a process by which we become more familiar with ourselves.

Stillness allows us to appreciate the present moment. We are able to reflect on our day to examine what went well and what could be improved upon. It is a means by which we process our thoughts and reconcile our feelings in a meaningful way. In this way, stillness enables self learning and development.

Apart from the psychological benefits of resting our minds from working on overdrive, stillness enables creativity. This is because it allows our minds to be free instead of being clogged with so much information and activity.

Stillness goes against the norm in today's world, where avoidance and escapism is the preferred option. It seems more comfortable for most people to be distracted by TV, social media, being in the company of friends etc. This is not to say that escapism is bad because it isn't. However, there's a time for welcoming distractions and a time for facing our thoughts and feelings. Avoiding our thoughts does not make them go away, they only get pushed down somewhere in our subconscious only to spring back up when we least expect.

An avoidant approach turns away from reality rather than towards it. In order to be effective players in our lives, we must learn to face reality, however hurtful it may be. In facing reality, we are able to develop the inner strength and emotional intelligence necessary to deal with life more effectively, thereby making life more manageable. For these reasons, it is healthier and more productive to learn to be alone with our thoughts. Our physical, psychological and emotional well-being will be the better for it.

Chapter 4. HOW TO LIVE A PURPOSEFUL LIFE

Face your fears

Fear is an emotion that prevents us from achieving success. It strips us of our self belief, thereby making us diffident and filled with self doubt. Fear makes our ideas remain in the mental state as it prevents their physical manifestation. Living in your head rather than living out your dreams is the product of fear. What's the worst that could really happen? Failure? It's better to make an attempt and fail than never giving it a shot. You really can't be certain until you try. We must not be scared to fail. In failing, we have the opportunity of learning more efficient ways of handling a situation. What's most important is taking calculated risks and diversifying our resources so that we have something to fall back on.

Duality is a recurring theme in life. Failure and success go hand in hand. This is because with the right attitude, failure can give us the opportunity to experiment with new methods and ideas, which can lead to an improved result and successful outcome.

It is perfectly understandable to feel sadness over failure. No one will be pleased to fail, after all. However, staying sad and stagnant is what should never happen. Instead, go over the processes that were undertaken, review them critically, seek advice if necessary and make adjustments where needed.

It is never too late to start over. It's important to note that the adherence to an idea shouldn't be simply borne out of stubbornness and pride. Amending errors and starting over can lead to success only when the path that has been towed is truly one in which our capabilities are aligned with and knowing this for certain can only come from self awareness and understanding the environment we are in.

Risks are an inherent part of life. As such, they cannot be avoided. Though risks are inevitable, it is sometimes possible to manage them so as to minimize their likelihood. Taking informed decisions, partnering with more knowledgeable stakeholders and spreading investments are some ways of managing risks.

On the other hand, just as the saying goes, you either go big or go home. As risks are a part of business, sometimes, when sufficient due diligence has been done, one can decide to take a bold step. Whatever the case may be, rash decisions should never be taken and diversification is necessary as it is never wise to put all your eggs in one basket.

Get uncomfortable

Being comfortable with our circumstances does not give us the incentive to change anything about them. Comfort is a state in which we are content to leave things as they are. While it is good to feel fulfilled about accomplishing our goals, it is unwise to rest on our laurels. Change is constant, nothing remains the same for too long. While we may feel that we have reached the zenith, with time, the target will certainly shift forward and there will be yet more goals to strive for. Therefore refusing to be comfortable should be the mentality we adopt so as to continuously challenge ourselves to attain even greater heights.

Another aspect of allowing yourself to be uncomfortable is doing what you are uncomfortable with to rid yourself of the fear associated with the activity. For example, if you're an introvert and the thought of socializing frightens you, you may want to face that fear head on. In doing so, you will come to realize that networking is not so daunting.

The ability to put ourselves in uncomfortable situations, not only challenges us to be greater achievers, it also enables us to face our fears. As a result, we learn more about ourselves and build confidence and self-esteem.

Don't wallow in regret

When we make mistakes, it is expected that we regret the decisions we took that led to the mistakes. It is perfectly normal to have feelings of regret as we are prone to making wrong judgement calls, which can be costly. Therefore, the problem is not occasionally having feelings of regret. Rather, it is allowing those feelings to consume us. When regret takes over us, we are unable to move forward and being stagnant for an indefinite period of time can lead to feelings of depression.

Wallowing in regret is an example of the adoption of a victim mentality, as discussed in the first part of the book. Emotional thinking cannot solve our problems so the expedient approach is to be rational by understanding why we made the erroneous decision, how to prevent such poor judgement in the future and finally, chucking the negative experience up to another of life's experiences that is intended to make us wiser and mentally stronger.

Free your mind

Don't feel bad about living life according to your terms.

Learn not to be judgemental. It is not profitable to make yourself judge over anybody. It is also unwise to judge what you do not fully comprehend. People should be free to choose the life they wish for themselves, provided that in doing so, there is no infringement on the rights of others. Also, don't look down on anyone as something can be learned from even the smallest of people.

Consuming yourself with hatred, envy and negativity does not foster growth, instead it leads to feelings of self worthlessness and anger. In order to be progressive, everything about you must be progressive, starting with the mind. A progressive mind admires and learns from successful people and seeks ways to adopt or adapt similar strategies to suit an objective. Hate, envy, blackmail and other such negativity is not part of its agenda because it recognizes the harm that these bring to progress.

Stay positive

Having a positive outlook is essential to having a successful life as we are likely to behave as we think. Being positive emanates from being confident and having self belief. Surrounding yourself with positive influences also helps in being positive. However, it's important to note that being positive without having the skills and capabilities necessary for being successful in your chosen career path is a waste. Positivity translates to success when we have the substance required to back it up.

Journey vs Destination

Just as we crawl before we walk, go through elementary school before high school, we must be willing and prepared to go through the right processes in order to achieve enduring success. We must also treat even the smallest opportunity with respect and gratitude. Humility, good work ethic and self motivation are all traits that must be imbibed in order to be successful.

We are usually so busy trying to get to the destination that we forget to enjoy the journey that gets us there. Most times, the journey is more important than the destination because oftentimes, there's no real destination. When we begin the journey, we may think that the destination is the attainment of a certain goal only to achieve the said goal and realize that we actually desire more. The target destination is ever evolving just as we are ever developing.

The journey is where the culmination of experiences takes place. It is also where self development takes place. Without the journey, there cannot be a destination. Therefore, the right mentality to have is to focus less on the destination and enjoy the journey. Enjoying the journey allows us to stay present. Staying present allows us to take notice of our daily achievements and improvements. It teaches us gratitude and appreciation of our progress, which makes us even more motivated to put in more effort so as to accomplish even more goals.

Put in the work

There is a price that we must pay for success. Enduring success does not come cheap. We must be ready to put in the work and time. We must also be ready to put on hold some of our other desires. For some this may be starting a family, while for some others it may be building a dream home or even going on vacation. Whatever it may be, as long as resources such as time and money are finite, there will always be an opportunity cost for achieving success.

Use your time wisely

Our time on earth is limited so it's imperative that we use it wisely. Spending our time on important activities, instead of dwelling on frivolities, will serve us better in the long run. Defining our goals and working towards them, rather than spending our time on group think and adopting a herd mentality, is a more beneficial way to maximize the use of our time.

Being disciplined and setting priorities helps in the productive use of our time. This is by no means suggesting that relaxation is a poor use of time. Escapism is necessary to relax our minds. It is the indulgence in escapism that becomes a distraction to our goals and objectives.

Moderation is always key in this regard.

Passion vs Money

When we make decisions about a career path, it is more profitable in the long run not to make financial benefit the central factor. It is expected that remuneration will play an important part in our decision making, however, following a career path solely because it attracts a large paycheck will likely backfire in the future.

Considering other factors such as opportunities for self development through courses and work shops, opportunities for travel, higher level of responsibility, ease of mobility within the organization, reputation of the organization and passion for career path should come before remuneration. This is because when we are passionate about a chosen career path that we are equally qualified for, we are able to add value to ourselves as well as to our work and with time, the financial benefits will follow.

Articulate your thoughts and desires

It is one thing to have impressive ideas, it's another to be able to articulate them so that they can be appreciated by others. The ability to articulate our thoughts effectively enables others to respond according to our desires. When we give clear orders, we can expect our subordinates to understand our vision and produce the desired results.

The ability to communicate effectively requires practice and precision.

Effective communication is a clear and concise way of relaying information, which leaves no room for misinterpretation. In order to be successful, we must be able to communicate with confidence and clarity to ensure that others are on the same page as we are. Being vague will only result in inconsistency, confusion, chaos and outright failure.

Innovate

Innovation is an important aspect of living a purposeful life. This is because it is a testament to our creativity, which is borne out of a need to constantly challenge ourselves. A creative person is one who is dilligent, focused and seeks to add value to themself and their environment at large. In order for a person to be creative, they cannot be complacent. There has to be a constant drive to do more. Such a person never feels comfortable and satisfied with the status quo. As such, we can say that a creative person is one who always seeks for improvement and development.

Understanding your environment

Our environment is the sum total of the factors that influence life within it. These include technological, social, political, legal and economic factors. A good understanding of our environment enables us harness our capabilities such that they can be monetized. It enables us plan efficiently while ensuring the effectiveness of our plans.

Having a thorough understanding of our environment is vital because a one size fits all approach cannot work. For example, what will work in Lagos may not work so well in Calabar as a result of the disparity in the socioeconomic make-up of the two cities.

Chapter 5. How Spirituality Facilitates Success

What is Spirituality?
There's a lot that we do, habits that we have developed, activities that we partake in, that we do not realize are aspects of spirituality. Perhaps this is because we tend to equate spirituality with religion, and so if an activity is not religious, we tend to ignore its spiritual connotations.
Spirituality is a concept that acknowledges a greater power and the ways in which we connect with this Higher Being. It involves more reliance on the unseen forces of nature and less on tangible, material things. Spirituality does not require that we follow any particular religion. It simply requires us to be open minded about life beyond the one we know.

What are the benefits of spirituality?
Spirituality concerns itself primarily with the importance of self awareness. It is a concept that teaches the connection to a Supreme Being through a knowledge of ourselves. The idea is that through self awareness, we will be able to discover our purpose.

Self development and self investment are also spiritual as they are processes through which we become better versions of ourselves physically, psychologically, emotionally, financially and spiritually. Self investment activities include health and fitness, professional courses, charitable works and mentoring.

Spirituality adjusts our focus and mentality from placing ourselves in the centre of things i.e. it enables us to be aware that the world does not revolve around us, thereby giving us a balanced view and a holistic approach towards life instead of a self-serving, myopic mentality.

Through the development of our spirituality, we are able to practice gratitude and understand the importance of giving back. We realize that our success doesn't count for much if we are not using the opportunities we have to pull others up. Service, in terms of mentoring and helping the less fortunate, will become a priority as we develop spiritually. This is because we begin to live by the principle that in order to receive more, we must give more of ourselves and our resources.

Spirituality promotes the law of cause and effect, i.e. it creates an awareness of there being consequences to our actions, good and bad alike. This understanding makes a spiritual person more likely to exude positivity because they realize that giving off good energy will return same to them.

A person who lives by the principle of cause and effect is one who would strive to be ethical in their business dealings. Such a person will be more inclined to put in the necessary work and adhere to the process required to develop themselves and become successful.

Another aspect of the promotion of cause and effect is the use of words of affirmation. This is basically the idea that we speak into existence what we desire to materialize in our lives. For example, speaking success into your place of business as you open for the day to bring about sales, customer satisfaction, customer retention, referrals, etc. The belief is that releasing positive energy returns positive energy our way.

A person who is rooted in spirituality is also likely to practice the law of intention. The law of intention is the idea that when we desire for an objective to be met, we visualize it as we intend for it to be and then work towards making our perceptions a reality. Sometimes, it can help to make the visualizations physical through the use of a dream board or vision board. A dream board is essentially a board, which comprises pictures of our dreams or visualizations. For example, if your objective is to buy a dream home or car, you can get a picture that resembles the home you want and a print out of the car and stick them onto the dream board. The idea is that seeing these items frequently will motivate us even more to work towards making their purchase a reality.

Spirituality teaches self responsibility, which is an essential aspect of self development and success. The knowledge that we have control over our words, thoughts, feelings, actions and inactions is extremely powerful because it enables us know that we have the power within us to change our circumstances. In this regard, spirituality promotes a victor mentality rather than a victim mentality.

The feelings of inner peace and happiness that we derive from having a spiritual life gives us the clarity of mind needed to receive inspiration and be creative. Meditation and a constant yearning for self knowledge allows us to understand ourselves better, thereby instilling the discipline to forge ahead with our goals in spite of the distractions that surround us. Meditation also reduces stress, lowers blood pressure, and generally, improves our well-being, which in turn makes us more energized to perform our duties at optimal levels.

There seems to be a misconception that in order to be truly spiritual, you have to forgo your material possessions and instead adopt an ascetic lifestyle. This is a fallacy because spirituality and wealth are not mutually exclusive. As a matter of fact, material abundance is a benefit of spirituality because spirituality is a concept that promotes growth and wholeness in every area of our lives. As such, a deeply spiritual person is expected to be whole not only spiritually (through self awareness and self investment) but also physically (through the enjoyment of good health), psychologically (through having a clear and sound mind) socially (through service to humanity and building relationships), emotionally (through having inner happiness and peace) and financially (through being wealthy).

Chapter 6. The Importance of Being Focused

What does it mean to be focused?

Focus is simply the ability to pay attention to things of value or importance and ignore those that are less important or distractions. Focus can also be referred to as attention or concentration. Focus is vital for all activities we partake in because without it, we will be unable to achieve anything.

How can being focused make us successful?

Saves Time

Focusing on a selective task, i.e. one task at a time, enables us to do it qualitatively and quickly. Zeroing our attention on that singular task facilitates efficiency and effectiveness.

Improves the quality of our lives

Being focused changes our lives for the better. As it is said, energy flows to where attention goes. Paying attention to our life goals causes our energies to be poured into activities that will help develop us hand steer us in the right path to achieving our objectives.

Self development

Focusing expands our knowledge and creates

opportunities that we didn't even realize existed. When we pay attention to self investment and development, we are bound to become more knowledgeable and aware of the existence of possibilities around us, thereby increasing the opportunities that are presented to us.

Increases Productivity

Focusing allows us to be more productive. This is because our time is spent wisely. Rather than get distracted by unimportant activities, we are able to invest our time on those that are vital to our growth and progression. When we are focused, we realize that we are able to accomplish a lot in less time. The speedy achievement of our goals then translates to the attainment of success in a shorter space of time.

Clarity of thought

Being focused allows us to think. Everything from self awareness, self development, problem solving, critical thinking, decision making, understanding and learning emanates from our ability to focus. Without the ability to concentrate, our minds will simply wander aimlessly and we will end up wasting time, or losing interest in our primary objectives.

Less Stress

Focusing our thoughts allows us to concentrate on less. As such, our minds are not weighed down with too much information and distractions. The ability to focus on less and produce more within a shorter time, allows us to perform our duties with less stress.

Connect with our subconscious mind

Focus is a vital aspect of meditation and stillness. As was discussed in an early section, stillness is the process through which we are able to connect with our inner selves for self awareness and self development purposes. It is also an activity through which we are able to process our thoughts and gain clarity about our feelings and experiences. The attainment of clarity of thought and a free mind, which lead to creativity, can be gotten only through being focused.

What are the disadvantages of losing focus?

Wastage of time

Constantly allowing our minds to wander or deviating our attention to distractions leads to a loss of time. We end up spending much longer to accomplish our tasks, which then leads to a delay in reaching our objectives and a slower path to success.

Errors/Failure

When our attention is divided, there is a higher chance that we will produce work that is riddled with errors and less impressive than we are capable of.

Poor quality of work

When we lack clarity of thought because we have allowed ourselves to be inundated with more information than is necessary, we will be unable to process our thoughts as well as we would have been able to. We will also be working under stressful conditions, thereby leading to the production of poor quality work.

Deviation from Purpose

The allowance of secondary objectives or unimportant activities to take over our lives leads to the deviation from our purpose. This is because we will be spending more time on these other activities than we should. This is time that would be taken away from our primary objectives. We should remember that what we give our attention to is what we grow.

Victim of herd mentality

When we do not have the self control necessary to focus on ourselves and avoid distractions, we end up being victims to whatever trends are popular and reliant on seeking the approval of others in order to validate ourselves.

What are the ways to increase our ability to focus?

Plan

The ability to be disciplined is necessary if we are to maintain focus. Creating schedules and adhering to them is an important aspect of being accountable to ourselves and our determination to follow the processes necessary to accomplish our goals.

Positive Attitude

A positive attitude is important to maintaining focus. It

enables us to forge ahead when faced with challenges or when we begin to have self doubt. Maintaining focus is difficult and it will test our mental strength. Positivity can sometimes be what makes the difference between continuing our paths and quitting.

Passion

It is important that we are passionate about our chosen paths as this is usually what keeps us going through difficult times. Having passion allows us to be consistent and resilient.

Pay Yourself

We must show appreciation and gratitude for our progress, no matter how inconsequential they may seem. Remember that small drops make a mighty ocean. When we make progress, we should celebrate it in a little way. The practice of rewarding ourselves serves as a boost to keep us pushing towards the realization of that big break.

Don't Procrastinate

Procrastination leads to a delay in our accomplishments. It usually happens because we have given room for distractions in our lives. Rather than procrastinate, plan towards your goals. The plan can include other activities that are secondary, albeit at a lower frequency than the primary objective. Making a plan that allows for other less important activities will enable you put off procrastinating.

Believe in Yourself

What we think is usually what we become. It's important to believe in our capabilities and to continually develop ourselves. The self belief we gain as a result of self improvement will enable us focus better and be goal-oriented.

Be practical

Being realistic about our goals is important to our ability to focus effectively on them. Our capabilities and qualifications must match our passion. Focusing on a goal without the requisite skills to make it a reality will produce no effect.

Create head space

Focusing is only possible when we are free from distractions.

Distractions can also come in the form of a clogged mind. We must learn to free our minds so as to create the head space necessary to think with clarity. Our minds can be relieved through meditation exercises. Making it a point of duty to frequently process our thoughts rather than avoid them goes a long way to relieving us from stress and anxiety. Focusing on less allows us to do more.

Delegate

There is no harm in delegating or seeking out assistance. However we can achieve the realization of our goals and prevent ourselves from being weighed down by stress or other feelings, that will serve as distractions and prevent us from being progressive, is encouraged.

Create an ordered workspace

Our workspace can be a source of distraction. Creating an ordered workspace is important because it allows us focus squarely on the objective at hand. A workspace that is cluttered cannot allow for optimum concentration and performance. Let your workspaces be a reflection of the headspaces that you require in order to be productive. Less is always better.

Avoid distractions

In today's digital world, a common source of distraction is technology. When we are focused on getting work done, it is better to either turn off our phones or divert unimportant calls. The television should also be turned off if we are to work efficiently and effectively. When we intend to work with our full attention, any potential source of distraction should be avoided.

How does focus lead to good leadership?

Focus is an important aspect of leadership. A leader should be able to focus inwardly, outwardly and on the global environment.

Inward Focus

A leader should be able to focus inwardly, as self awareness is key. Self awareness enables a leader make better decisions. Self awareness also contributes to our development of self control.

Outward Focus

An ability to focus outwardly enables a leader build social relationships and have empathy. An outward focus enables the leader understand how to maximize the potentials of others, understand their perspectives and feelings, and makes them aware of what others require of them. A leader that is able to have empathy and social sensitivity is one who gains the respect of his subordinates, whose opinion matters a great deal to others and for whom others are motivated to work diligently.

This type of leader will also make a good mentor.

Focus on the Global Environment

Focusing on the global environment is important because it enables the leader devise strategies, which ensure that the company is able to be innovative and remain competitive and profitable. Utmost concentration is required to exploit existing opportunities as well as to seek new ones. A leader who is able to focus on the world at-large is one who is open minded, inquisitive, a good listener and also a visionary.

As has been explained, it is clear that focus is a key aspect of building leadership skills. Focus should be on every aspect of the organization and not just on a select few or on those parts that are deemed more important. Attention is the basis of emotional, organizational and strategic excellence, so it cannot be compromised.

Chapter 7. NETWORKING AND MENTORING

What is networking?

Networking is a social activity through which we develop mutually beneficial relationships. The aim of networking is to build new relationships as well as strengthen existing relationships. Trust is an important factor in networking. Trusting others and gaining the trust of others is vital because a relationship without trust cannot be built on.

What are the benefits of networking?

Strengthen business connections

Through meeting new people and developing new relationships or strengthening existing ones, we are able to create or deepen our connections. Who you know as opposed to what you know plays a huge role in determining success. Networking opens us up to forging relationships with those we may not have had access to ordinarily. Not only do we develop a relationship with new contacts, we also have the opportunity to tap into the network of our new acquaintances as well, thereby broadening our connections even further.

Generate new ideas

The exposure to new people with varied levels of exposure and expertise can lead to us learning new methods and processes of achieving our goals and objectives. Conversing with new people generally broadens our horizons, which can lead to the generation of new ideas.

Increase Knowledge

We are able to tap into the minds of our new contacts and ask them for advice and suggestions, which gives us a deeper insight and makes us more knowledgeable.

Advance Career

Through networking, we have the opportunity of meeting different people of influence and in positions of power who are able to offer us referrals and provide us with avenues for business, career or personal growth.

Advice and Mentoring

Networking is a mutually beneficial exchange where people feel free to discuss with like-minded individuals and seek inspiration and direction from those who are more knowledgeable.

Confidence

Walking up to total strangers is not easy, especially for those who are shy or introverted. It requires confidence and courage to approach a stranger and strike a meaningful conversation with them. The ability to be successful at networking builds up your self esteem and enables you conquer your fears of rejection.

Friendships

Networking is an avenue through which we are able to build meaningful friendships. There is a camaraderie that develops when we engage with individuals who are willing to offer their knowledge and support to us. Trust is built through such interactions and the nature of the relationship organically transforms from acquaintance to friendship.

Positive Influence

The intention of networking is to create a positive atmosphere in which qualitative interactions can be made. The support, knowledge, connections, mentoring and development gained through networking makes it a positive influence on our personal and professional lives.

Raise your Profile

Networking is a good way to build a reputation. Keeping a busy social calendar and having positive and memorable interactions enables others remember you. Through recognition, referrals can begin to be made in your favor.

Satisfaction from helping others

Networking provides the opportunity for those who have a passion for helping others to meet less experienced people, who are inquisitive, passionate about their careers and seeking out mentors.

HOW TO NETWORK EFFICIENTLY

Diversify your events

Attending various types of events is important as this will

increase the likelihood of meeting different sets of people. The broader our network is, the more opportunities we are presented with.

Leverage your social media networks
Social media is a tool that can be used to network, if used effectively. Through social media, we have access to our networks as well as those of our connections.

Meet people through referrals
As mentioned earlier, networking allows us to tap into the connections of our connections. To effectively network, we must explore every opportunity as the aim is to make as many meaningful connections as possible.

Help your Network
Networking is a give and take situation. It is preferable to give before you make any requests. Be a valuable member of your network by offering your time, sharing your knowledge and providing support and motivation to others. Doing these help build trust and a good reputation.

Build genuine relationships
The priority should always be to serve as a positive influence to others. Once we are recognized for the value we add, others will be more likely to reciprocate by offering themselves to us. Being seen as trustworthy enables the building of genuine relationships with others.

Be courageous and confident
People naturally gravitate towards those who carry themselves with confidence and exude success. It is

important you represent what you want others to think about you. However, this is not to mean that we should be inauthentic by living beyond our means. It simply means that we should be the embodiment of confidence, courtesy and positivity.

Make your interactions rewarding and positive

A rewarding and positive interaction cannot easily be forgotten. In order for others to remember you and wish to build a relationship with you, you must stand out in a positive way. Ensure that you speak intelligently, ask the right questions, proffer clever suggestions, listen attentively, and generally, have a positive aura.

Stay in Touch

Keeping in contact with our new contacts is important to keeping ourselves relevant in their minds. Relationships cannot be built when we meet people and forget about them soon after. Keeping in touch lets them know that they are valuable to us.

Don't be quick to ask for favors

No one likes a user. As much as you may have partaken in networking because you are seeking a job, for example, do not let desperation cause you to be quick to ask for favors. Rather, focus on meeting new people and building genuine bonds, enjoying the general atmosphere, learning from the knowledge being shared and advice received, and that job will find you before you realize it.

Have a pleasant appearance

Proper grooming is essential at all times, most especially

when we are engaging in social interactions. The first impression we make is crucial when meeting new people. A pleasing appearance gives us the confidence to navigate social events with self assurance. It attracts people to us easily, thereby making developing relationships easier. As was mentioned in the first part of the book, a good appearance is capable of opening doors that would otherwise have been shut.

Who are mentors?

Mentors are more experienced individuals who help guide less experienced folk through building trust and leading by example. They help by identifying and developing the skills necessary for the attainment of goals and objectives. A mentor invests in the life of others by giving tips, support, advice and motivation.

The individual being mentored, on the other hand, is able to improve their performance through being motivated and putting the advice received into use. The improvement in self esteem and confidence is also gained through the achievement of a better performance, skill acquisition or development and moral support.

Sometimes, professional mentors end up as life coaches because it can be difficult to separate professional from personal growth.

WHAT ARE THE BENEFITS OF MENTORING?

Mentoring is an example of networking so some of it's benefits are similar to those of networking.

Mentoring broadens our horizons by providing us with new perspectives and suggestions.

We are able to seek advice without feeling self-conscious or ashamed.

Through knowledge acquisition, mentoring enables us improve our skills, develop our expertise and gives us the confidence and self belief needed to improve ourselves.

Mentors provide the moral support and motivation necessary to keep us moving forward along our career paths.

Mentors expand our networks by providing us with access to their own networks.

Through the guidance of a mentor, we are able to avoid making mistakes that would otherwise have been made. This in turn saves our time and other valuable resources.

The bond with a mentor, based on genuine care, good will and trust, serves as the basis for a long-lasting friendship.

Mentoring is an opportunity to give back to society by providing an avenue to lift others up and being the catalyst for change and improvement in their lives.

No man is an island. Humans are social creatures, so we have the propensity to create bonds and grow through our relationships with others. It's important to seek inspiration and knowledge from others as it helps in our process of development, both personally and professionally. In seeking advice and expanding our social circles, the consideration should always be value addition and positive influence.

Chapter 8. LIFE IS A PROCESS

How is life a process?

Life being a process simply means that it comprises several stages that contribute to our development. We all grow, develop and mature and as we do, we transition from one stage to another.

It also means that life is a journey. The process of life is the sum total of all the experiences we have on our journey of self discovery and actualization. Every part of the process is important because they play a part in our development. For this reason, we must endeavour to stay present in each stage and enjoy the journey.

How to ensure a successful life journey

Set SMART objectives

Setting smart objectives is essential to enabling us be successful. SMART is an acronym, which stands for specific, measurable, attainable, relevant and time-bound

Specific goals: These are precise goals. We must ensure that our goals are properly defined.

Measurable goals: The clear and concise nature of specific goals enables us measure our success in achieving them.

Attainable goals: Our goals must be realistic. In setting

goals, we must be practical rather than over ambitious. We must set goals that we have the capabilities of achieving. Knowing that we have the skills necessary to achieve our goals gives us the drive to pursue them.

Relevant goals: Our goals must pertain to our chosen career path or be in line with the achievement of our main objectives.

Time-bound: Setting a deadline for our goals makes us accountable for them. It makes us disciplined and causes us to use our time wisely.

Break down your objectives

It's important to break our goals into smaller goals so that we do not feel overwhelmed by them. In minimizing a big goal to several smaller goals, we are able to celebrate our small victories, which serves as motivation to keep us working towards the attainment of our main goal.

Become masters over your distractions

We need to be realistic about our weaknesses. Finding out what our major source of distractions are helps us to consciously minimize the time we spend on them. For example, if you enjoy watching TV shows, you can allocate some time to enjoy watching a couple of your favourite shows. The idea is that allowing some time to your distraction instead of denying yourself, will prevent them from getting in the way of you focusing on your objectives.

Make out time for yourself

Regardless of how busy we get, we must make time out for working towards our goals. It may even be as little as 30 minutes daily. Whatever the case, it is essential that we have a routine to keep us along a progressive path.

Reflect on your journey and progress

Constant reflection reminds us of the importance of our goals. It also allows us to assess areas we may need to improve upon as well as acknowledge our progress.

Enjoy the process

Having a positive outlook and making the process enjoyable makes it easier to continue along a progressive path because we are not overcome with feelings of stress or anxiety. Having fun and being positive also allows inspiration and creativity to flow more readily.

Growth and development are integral parts of life. Just as we crawl before we are able to walk and then run, success is not instantaneous.

The journey or processes involved in the achievement of success are just as important as the goal itself. As such, character building and the inculcation of positive values and virtues such as patience,

perseverance, resilience and humility are vital to our success stories. Our attitudes definitely determine how high we soar and for how long we keep soaring.

Chapter 9. EMOTIONAL INTELLIGENCE

What are positive emotions?

Positive emotions are those that we find pleasurable to experience. Examples are happiness and peacefulness. These feelings encourage us to become better versions of ourselves by boosting our self esteem and self belief.

What are the benefits of positive emotions?
Positive emotions broaden our ability to learn and think. This is because they encourage self motivation and self assertion, which enables us perform optimally.
They give us the ability to be resilient when faced with unpleasant circumstances. They serve as a coping mechanism against negative circumstances and prevent negative emotions from overwhelming us.
Positive emotions improve our well-being and our ability to interact with others, thereby enhancing our social skills and ability to contribute to our environment.

What are negative emotions?
Negative emotions are those that we do not find pleasurable to experience. These are feelings that discourages us and puts us in a bad mood. Examples are anger, frustration, fear, loneliness etc. Negative emotions

can dampen our lives by making us lose motivation. They can also distort our perception of reality by causing us to focus on the negative aspects of life. Hence, we begin to see the glass as half empty rather than half full. Experiencing negative emotions over a sustained period of time can lead to depression.

How to manage negative emotions

Self reflection

The ability to be introspective, through meditation, is important in enabling us manage negative emotions effectively. Figuring out what we feel is the first step towards understanding the emotion.

Acknowledging the emotion

Once we are able to understand what we feel by naming the emotion, we can begin to understand why we feel the way we do, what to do to manage the feelings and how to channel the emotion positively.

Don't be hard on yourself

Self compassion is important here. We must realize that there is nothing abnormal about negative emotions so there is no need to be hard on ourselves. They are only detrimental when we channel them wrongly and remain in a negative state.

Compassion

Oftentimes, the best way to relieve ourselves of negative feelings is by showing compassion to others. Giving of our time, in whichever way we can, helps us focus less on the negative feelings and gives us a different perspective. Recognizing that we are in a better position, as compared to many others, teaches us gratitude. Appreciation for the things we have can help relieve us of negative feelings.

Exercise

Engaging in exercise, can help lift our spirits and make us feel good about ourselves, which in turn will lessen or eradicate the negative feelings.

Escapism

Distractions are a welcome idea here. Focusing on our hobbies, watching a movie or any form of relaxation we enjoy, can get our minds off ruminating on the negative thoughts and feelings.

Share your thoughts

It helps to speak with a trusted friend or professional. They may be able to offer us a different perspective and words of wisdom, which would enable us deal with the emotions in a constructive manner. Also, speaking about our feelings helps lessen their effect on us. As it is said, a problem shared is a problem halved.

Count your blessings

Being grateful for the good things in our life helps us put things in the proper perspective. To focus all our energies on negativity, when we have so much to be grateful for, is an unprofitable way to live.

Learn to let go

Letting go of our past hurt helps rid us of the negative

emotions that weigh us down. It also allows us to appreciate the present. It's important to avoid dwelling on the situation that brought about the negative emotion as this would only exacerbate the feelings. Freeing ourselves of the guilt or sadness attached to negative emotions enables us to truly feel emancipated and reborn.

Declutter your life

Get rid of every source of stress in your life. These are also responsible for triggering negative emotions. These may include negative influences, negative habits and toxic relationships.

What are the benefits of negative emotions?

Negative emotions can serve as an opportunity for self development. We can channel our negative emotions in order to produce positive results in our lives. Accepting that they are a normal aspect of life should make us see them as a means of learning more about ourselves and an opportunity for growth and development.

Negative emotions can be beneficial because they can serve as a means of survival and the encouragement we need to develop our potentials. For example, fear prevents us from dangerous situations, anger helps us fight against our problems and disgust helps us reject those things that are unhealthy or negative influences in our lives.

Sometimes, it takes us being in a low emotional and psychological state to connect with the deepest part of ourselves. As such, negative emotions can lead us to self discovery and development, developing feelings of empathy and humility, as well as making us open-minded and less judgemental.

Both positive and negative emotions are important to feel as each have their benefits. As duality is a recurring theme in life, one cannot exist without the other. Our ability to accept and exploit both positive and negative emotions enables us live balanced and meaningful lives.

What is emotional intelligence?

Emotional intelligence is the capacity to recognize and manage our emotions as well as those of others around us. It is also referred to as emotional quotient or EQ.

Emotional intelligence consists of four parts: perceiving emotions, understanding emotions, managing emotions and using emotions to facilitate thinking.

Perceiving emotions is the ability to identify meanings in body language, facial expressions and tone of voice. It is the ability to read between the lines and understand covert messages from those around us.

Understanding emotions is the ability to makes sense of the emotions we perceive. It is concerned with translating the messages that were perceived.

Using emotions to facilitate thinking is important to our abilities to having a positive mind-set. It is about utilizing our emotions to serve us rather than cause us to self destruct e.g. focusing on directing our emotions towards problem solving, decision-making, creative pursuits etc. Managing emotions is about developing self control and not allowing our feelings to dictate our actions. There are many benefits associated with our ability to mange our emotions. Some are the development of our mental strength, ability to overcome challenges and peace of mind.

How does emotional intelligence contribute to success?

Being emotionally intelligent helps with self control. The ability to keep our composure gives us the clearness of thought and presence of mind necessary in such activities as strategic thinking and decision making.

The empathy we have by being emotionally intelligent makes it easier for us to show compassion for others and be socially sensitive. A socially sensitive person is able to develop meaningful relationships with others, communicate effectively and be a good team player.

Emotional intelligence creates self awareness, which helps with self development and a continuous effort towards self improvement.

The awareness of others is another benefit of emotional intelligence. This translates to the ability to motivate others, resolve conflict, and harness the strengths of others so as to contribute to success.

Chapter 10. Financial Intelligence

What is financial intelligence?
Financial intelligence is the knowledge and skills gained from our understanding of finance.

What is the importance of financial responsibility?

Increase wealth
Keeping track of your cash flow to know where money is going and coming from enables you assess ways to modify or eliminate certain items being spent on.

Improves our relationship with money
It allows us to realize that we need to be in control of our money, rather than it being in control of us. Budgeting and planning becomes easy when we are able to control our money.

Improves our knowledge of money
We become better informed about assets and liabilities, which helps us make better financial decisions and avoid debt.

Informs what we spend on
It exposes us to ways in which our money can work for us through investments and imbibing a savings culture. In other words, financial intelligence teaches us financial

prudence.

Gives us insights into financial markets

Knowledge about financial markets enables us know when it is best to make investments and which investments are best to make at certain times. This facilitates our ability to grow wealth more easily.

How being a good money manager can lead to business success

Setting short and long term goals

Differentiating your goals according to long and short term enables you stay focused and balanced, which in turn contributes to your ability to be successful.

Hiring and/or networking with financially intelligent people

Mingling with good money managers increases our knowledge, skills and insights about finance, which helps us become better money managers.

Taking responsibility for poor decisions

Self responsibility and learning from our mistakes contributes to our self development. It also gives an insight into better strategies to adopt in order to make more favorable financial decisions.

Planning/Budgeting

Having a comprehensive plan that you manage and implement on a daily basis keeps you accountable to yourself and helps you stay on a steady path to accomplishing both short and long term goals.

Saving a portion of your income

Adopting a culture of saving is important to being a successful money manager. The ability to be disciplined and prudent with our resources is an essential aspect to our ability to grow wealth.

Minimizing your purchasing of liabilities

The knowledge of the difference between assets and liabilities enables us make better financial decisions. Limiting our spending on liabilities prevents us from accruing debt, which is a major contributing factor of stunted progress.

Spending money strategically

It's important to avoid making impulse purchases, however small, as they can add up to having an effect on our abilities to execute our long term plans. The importance of being disciplined cannot be overstated.

Foresight

The ability to determine if the likely consequences of an investment will be favorable or unfavorable in the long run enables us take calculated risks, which is an essential aspect to achieving success.

Learning

Seeking information should be never-ending. There is no

room for complacency on the path to success. We must make the acquisition of knowledge about money a lifestyle by reading books, journals, magazines, watching television stations and listening to radio programs dedicated to finance. These outlets will give us more insight about money, investments, properties and the stock market. Having a deeper insight helps us devise better strategies and exploit more opportunities, which contributes to our abilities to be innovative, competitive and profitable.

Ayn Rand sums up the importance of financial intelligence to success succinctly when he said, "Wealth is the product of a man's capability to think". In saying this, he meant that the ability to gain wealth is a product of our mentality about money. Intelligence solves problems, not money. A lack of knowledge, discipline and focus can make a person go from riches to rags. Conversely, having these attributes can make a person go from rags to riches.

connect With Author

Connect with Adetunbi Whose mission is to promote a positive philosophy of leadership,power of the people and ability to change their lives and gerneration. www.adetunbiowo.com. You can send a message via Whatsapp +2348147931498

Conclution.

Though it's easier said than done, achieving success is by no means unattainable. We have so many testimonies around us to attest to the plausibility of living a purposeful and successful life. On the path to success, it's important to note that success is a personal journey. What matters most is that we are authentic, progressive and content with the choices we make.

A realistic approach to life cannot be overemphasized. When we approach life with a practical mentality, we are better able to face the challenges that come our way and are more mentally prepared for achieving enduring success.

We must strive to constantly get to know ourselves and what we want out of life. Sometimes, it's easier to define what we want out of life by clarifying those things that we do not want. These will inform our decisions about what a fulfilling life looks like.

In the pursuit of a purposeful life, we will realize that being focused is extremely beneficial. We must be intentional about the activites that we are involved in and the relationships we keep; the fewer the distractions, the better. In living a purposeful life, the emphasis should be placed on value addition. What does not add value to us as people or our careers is a distraction and therefore, should be done away with. However, this is not to say that we should only be involved in serious-minded activities. Entertainment also adds value to us by relieving us from feelings of stress as well as by providing enjoyment and imparting knowledge. However, we must remember to avoid overindulgence; moderation is always key.

 Life is a process. It is a journey that is forever evolving as we also evolve as humans. Our needs and desires, which inform what success is to us, also evolve with time. What we wanted as teenagers is different to what we want in the various stages of adulthood. As such, self learning and introspection should be a continuous process.

Our paths to success is also a process. We must be willing to pay our dues and remain present in the process rather than constantly looking forward to the finish line. The perceived finish line is an illusion as it keeps shifting while the actual finish line is not one we wish to look forward to because our journeys only truly come to an end with death. Spirituality is an important aspect in the lives of many people. It is the belief in a higher, more powerful life force.

Spirituality is an aspect of a lot of activities we partake in without us even realizing it. Some examples of spiritual practices are meditation, self development, mentoring, charitable works, ethical business practices, positive thinking etc. These are all aspects to attaining success financially as well as emotionally, psychologically and physically.

Our abilities to manage our emotions, good and bad, puts us in a position to manage success efficiently. Managing good emotions enables us to maintain focus and prevents us from getting ahead of ourselves or premature celebrations and pronounciations of success. Managing bad emotions also enables us maintain focus and prevents challenges from getting the better of us. Managing our emotions effectively also enables us to resist distractions and overcome setbacks. Being emotionally intelligent develops us in terms of maturity, patience, perseverance, discretion, diplomacy and discipline.

Being responsible and prudent with our finances helps tremendously on our paths to success. Recognizing the difference between wants and needs as well as between assets and liabilities helps curtail our spending on frivolities and instead, keeps us focused on investing in profitable ventures, which will grow our wealth.

In spite of hardships, we must continually strive to better ourselves in every area of our lives. We owe ourselves that much. We must indulge ourselves in continuous learning and development, as this will equip us with the knowlege and skills to do more and be more.

It's important to note that learning and development should not be limited to those gotten through formal education. The experiences through which we learn about ourselves and life, in general, mostly happen outside the classroom. Therefore, we must not discount the importance of informal education.

Remember that life is a process and all we have to do is start by placing one foot in front of the other. As long as we are moving in the right direction, improvement is certain and with time, success will be within our grasp.